Dear Parents:

Congratulations! Your child is taking
the first steps on an exciting journey.
The destination? Independent reading!

STEP INTO READING® will help your child get there. The program offers
five steps to reading success. Each step includes fun stories and colorful
art or photographs. In addition to original fiction and books with favorite
characters, there are Step into Reading Non-Fiction Readers, Phonics Readers
and Boxed Sets, Sticker Readers, and Comic Readers—a complete literacy
program with something to interest every child.

Learning to Read, Step by Step!

Ready to Read   Preschool–Kindergarten
• big type and easy words • rhyme and rhythm • picture clues
For children who know the alphabet and are eager to
begin reading.

Reading with Help   Preschool–Grade 1
• basic vocabulary • short sentences • simple stories
For children who recognize familiar words and sound out
new words with help.

Reading on Your Own   Grades 1–3
• engaging characters • easy-to-follow plots • popular topics
For children who are ready to read on their own.

Reading Paragraphs   Grades 2–3
• challenging vocabulary • short paragraphs • exciting stories
For newly independent readers who read simple sentences
with confidence.

Ready for Chapters   Grades 2–4
• chapters • longer paragraphs • full-color art
For children who want to take the plunge into chapter books
but still like colorful pictures.

STEP INTO READING® is designed to give every child a successful
reading experience. The grade levels are only guides; children will progress
through the steps at their own speed, developing confidence in their reading.

Remember, a lifetime love of reading starts with a single step!

Visit us on the Web!
StepIntoReading.com
rhcbooks.com

Educators and librarians, for a variety of teaching tools, visit us at RHTeachersLibrarians.com

ISBN 978-0-593-64601-4 (trade) — ISBN 978-0-593-64602-1 (lib. bdg.)

Printed in the United States of America

10 9 8 7 6 5 4 3 2 1

Mario's Big Adventure

by Mary Man-Kong

Random House 🏠 New York

This is Bowser.

He is the King of the Koopas

and rules over an army of evil turtles.

He breathes fire and wants

to attack other kingdoms.

Bowser has found the

Super Star.

This Power-Up makes

you invincible!

Bowser wants to use the

Super Star to rule the

Mushroom Kingdom!

This is Mario.

He is a plumber who lives

in Brooklyn, New York.

He is confident and brave

and wants to be

the best plumber ever!

Mario helps people

wherever he goes.

No job—or pipe—

is too small or too big

for our hero.

Luigi is Mario's brother.

He is always ready to lend a hand.

Sometimes Luigi gets scared,

but he tries to be brave.

Luigi and Mario ride in an orange van.
They work together as a team at the
Super Mario Bros. Plumbing Company.

Mario and Luigi discover
a special pipe beneath Brooklyn.
The pipe leads Mario to
the Mushroom Kingdom.

Mario meets Toad
while looking for his brother.
Mario asks Toad to
to help him find Luigi.
Toad knows who can help!

Luigi gets pulled into

a different kingdom.

He finds himself in a dark world.

Luigi walks to an old house.

It is a haunted castle!

Luigi is very afraid.

Toad is fearless and loyal
to Princess Peach.
She is the ruler of the
Mushroom Kingdom.
When Princess Peach
was young,
the toads raised her.
Now she defends
them all!

Mario meets Princess Peach and learns that the Mushroom Kingdom is in danger!
Mario offers to help.

Princess Peach trains Mario
and teaches him about
the special abilities of
Power-Ups.

Bowser's henchmen catch Luigi
and bring him to Bowser's airship.
Bowser tries to get information
about Mario.
Luigi does not tell him anything,
so Bowser puts Luigi in jail.

Princess Peach believes they will
need the help of the Jungle Kingdom.
She and Mario decide to go there.
Toad goes with them.

King Cranky Kong is the ruler
of the Jungle Kingdom.
King Cranky Kong says that
if they want his help,
Mario must beat his son
in the Great Ring of Kong.

Donkey Kong is

Cranky Kong's son.

He is a very strong warrior,

but he sometimes acts like a child.

Donkey Kong hopes

to be a good leader one day.

Donkey Kong loves
to throw barrels
and smash things.
He is very strong!

He battles Mario in the

Great Ring of Kong.

Mario makes full use of

Power-Ups to fight Donkey Kong.

Mario and his friends need
to catch and defeat Bowser.
Princess Peach designs
an amazing pink motorbike.

Mario creates a red Kart
that is built for speed.
And Donkey Kong builds a
powerful green and yellow Kart.

Mario and his friends
are ready to save the day.
Here we go!